Published by UpLit Press, UK
First Edition 2023

A Fox Named Fergus

Written and illustrated by

Jenny Canning

Can you find all the places Monty the mouse is hiding?

There once was a
fox named Fergus

Who was unusually
uneasy and
nervous.

His mummy and daddy couldn't understand what was wrong.

He wouldn't eat meat and felt he didn't belong.

The day came for Fergus
to prove he could hunt,

So mummy and daddy sent him
down to the waterfront.

Fergus felt confused,
there was something not right,

But if he took home no meat,
they would be hungry all night.

Ahead in a beautiful meadow,
a rabbit hopped happily free.

Fergus wanted to go further,
but wasn't meant to go as far
as the big pink tree.

On the ground he spotted a carrot the rabbit had left behind.

Fergus was tempted and gave it a try. Something felt right, soothing his mind.

The rabbit hopped over, unthreatened by the sight.

"I'm Rufus," he said as he smiled with delight.

"It's unusual to see a fox
who doesn't eat meat.

Come see our burrow,
it's awfully neat."

Fergus was enchanted by what he was seeing.

He had finally discovered his reason for being.

Rufus told mummy rabbit not to be scared.

"Fergus is just like us," he declared.

Mummy rabbit gave him a carrot to take home for tea.

A sense of belonging made him hop away with glee.

Fergus started thinking what
more he could do.

If he became more "rabbit"
he would stop feeling blue.

He curled up his tail and hopped into the wood

In search of adornments to help him feel good.

Leaves would be perfect for long rabbit ears.

He tied them on with grass, happier than he'd been in years.

He pulled two petals from a pretty white flower.

Collecting sticky sap he felt a sense of great power.

Sticking the petals on his sharp pointy teeth,

He expressed outside what he felt underneath.

Only one last step to feeling complete:
A little pink nose like Rufus's
would be sweet.

He hopped on some berries
to crush them up fine.
Rubbing his nose in them,
he started to shine.

Fergus was excited to show his true self to his friend.

He hopped back to the meadow with his mind on the mend.

From the edge of the grass, a little voice tittered.

It was Monty the mouse, mean and embittered.

Monty sniggered, "A fox who's a rabbit, what a ridiculous sight.

It's silly, it's mad, it's clearly not right."

Feeling upset, Fergus sought comfort at home.

He knew mummy and daddy would stop him feeling so alone.

But then he remembered: he's a rabbit now.

He needed to tell them but didn't know how.

Mummy and daddy liked rabbits in pie.

But he felt so happy he didn't want to lie.

Fergus explained, "I've known for a while that something wasn't right.

I've been feeling so sad and I couldn't find the light.

I feel so much better now living this way.

A rabbit is what I want to be every day.

I hope you understand, a fox is not what I am.

I belong in a burrow, and I hate eating ham."

Fergus broke down in tears, upset
that Monty had laughed and judged.

He hoped his parents would support
him, but their opinion on rabbits
would not be budged.

Mummy fox cuddled Fergus and told him she would always be there for her son.

Daddy fox was furious and told Fergus he was done.

Fergus was heartbroken and ran away to the meadow.

"Please help me," he cried to Rufus, "I have nowhere to go."

Rufus and mummy rabbit welcomed Fergus with hops and jumps.

They hugged him and stopped him being down in the dumps.

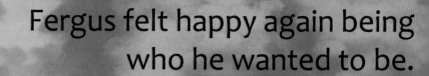

Fergus felt happy again being
who he wanted to be.

Mummy and daddy fox saw him
hopping happy and free.

They saw how important it was
for their son to be content.

Now they realised how much
supporting him meant.

So they changed their views for the
love of their child.

They said, "We support you, Fergus,"
and he lovingly smiled.

There once was a rabbit named Fergus.

He was a very happy rabbit.

About the Author

My name is Jenny Canning. For the majority of my life, I have been actively involved in LGBTQ+ society, specifically the trans community, both professionally and personally, offering support and understanding, cosmetics and style advice through my work as a makeup artist. As part of my masters in creative practice, I have taken the opportunity to extend my support by writing and illustrating this story.

Witnessing the difficulties that anybody who expresses themselves differently comes across motivated me to create this book. Thank you to my Leeds First Friday family and my personal family for inspiring me to write this story.

Printed in Great Britain
by Amazon

23319419R00016